WOULD YOU DARE?

WOULD YOU DARE FLY A FIGHTER JET?

By Robert Kennedy

HOT TOPICS

Gareth Stevens
PUBLISHING

Please visit our website, www.garethstevens.com. For a free color catalog of all our high-quality books, call toll free 1-800-542-2595 or fax 1-877-542-2596.

Cataloging-In-Publication Data

Names: Kennedy, Robert.
Title: Would you dare fly a fighter jet? / Robert Kennedy.
Description: New York : PowerKids Press, 2017. | Series: Would you dare? | Includes index.
Identifiers: ISBN 9781482458107 (pbk.) | ISBN 9781482458121 (library bound) | ISBN 9781482458114 (6 pack)
Subjects: LCSH: Fighter planes--Juvenile literature. | Fighter planes--Piloting--Juvenile literature.
Classification: LCC UG1242.F5 K46 2017 | DDC 623.74'64--d23

First Edition

Published in 2017 by
Gareth Stevens Publishing
111 East 14th Street, Suite 349
New York, NY 10003

Copyright © 2017 Gareth Stevens Publishing

Designer: Laura Bowen
Editor: Therese Shea

Photo credits: Cover, p. 1 (fighter pilot) SergioJPadronA/Moment Select/Getty Images; cover, pp. 1–32 (background) Nik Merkulov/Shutterstock.com; cover, pp. 1–32 (paint splat) Milan M/Shutterstock.com; cover, pp. 1–32 (photo frame) Milos Djapovic/Shutterstock.com; p. 5 (passenger plane) IM_photo/Shutterstock.com; p. 5 (F-15) Curioushavedape/Wikimedia Commons; p. 7 Stocktrek/DigitalVision/Getty Images; p. 8 Fæ/Wikimedia Commons; p. 9 (main) Paul Drabot/Shutterstock.com; p. 9 (inset) Mark Schierbecker/Wikimedia Commons; p. 11 Aviatrix8704/Wikimedia Commons; p. 13 Steve Mann/Shutterstock.com; pp. 14, 17 Chris Parypa Photography/Shutterstock.com; p. 15 Knumina Studios/Shutterstock.com; p. 16 arda savasciogullari/Shutterstock.com; p. 19 (main) Douglas Peebles/Corbis Documentary/Getty Images; p. 19 (inset) Matanya/Wikimedia Commons; p. 21 Aero Graphics, Inc./Corbis Documentary/Getty Images; p. 22 Archive Photos/Hulton Archive/Getty Images; p. 23 bibiphoto/Shutterstock.com; p. 25 FRED TANNEAU/AFP/Getty Images; p. 26 Head/Wikimedia Commons; p. 27 pryzmat/Shutterstock.com; p. 29 Jaroslav Moravcik/Shutterstock.com; p. 30 (Lightning) MathKnight/Wikimedia Commons; p. 30 (F-15) Hashekemist/Wikimedia Commons; p. 30 (Sukhol) Chanakyathegreat-commonswiki/Wikimedia Commons; p. 30 (Mikoyan) MODfoto/Wikimedia Commons; p. 30 (Lockheed) Balmung0731/Wikimedia Commons; p. 30 (Blackbird) Revent/Wikimedia Commons; p. 30 (X-15) Cooper.ch/Wikimedia Commons.

All rights reserved. No part of this book may be reproduced in any form without permission in writing from the publisher, except by a reviewer.

Printed in the United States of America

CPSIA compliance information: Batch #CW17GS: For further information contact Gareth Stevens, New York, New York at 1-800-542-2595.

CONTENTS

Ready for Takeoff	4
What Is a Fighter Jet?	6
Who Flies Fighter Jets?	10
The Speed of Sound	12
Catapulted!	18
Fighting Forces	20
Ejection Seat	24
Are You Ready?	28
For More Information	31
Glossary	32
Index	32

READY FOR TAKEOFF

Riding in an airplane is usually a calm **experience**. Once it climbs into the air, you can barely tell you're moving. A fighter jet is totally different. You can tell you're moving for sure—and moving fast!

passenger plane

F-15 fighter jet

DARING DATA

The fighter jet called the F-15 can fly about 1,900 miles (3,058 km) per hour!

WHAT IS A FIGHTER JET?

Fighter jets are planes used mostly for fighting other planes in the sky. That's why they're made to go so fast. They have to maneuver, or change course, quickly to surprise the enemy and stay safe from harm.

DARING DATA

Some jets are also used to drop **bombs** or fight objects on the ground.

Fighter jets have jet engines. Jet engines release, or let free, gases in a powerful way. The jets of gas shoot backward, and the whole plane is pushed forward. That creates thrust, the force that drives aircraft forward.

jet engine test run

DARING DATA

The air in jet engines can reach 3,000°F (1,649°C)!

WHO FLIES FIGHTER JETS?

In the United States, fighter pilots serve in the air force, navy, and marines. Not everyone can be a pilot. Pilots must have very good eyesight and perfect hearing. They must go through many weeks of flight training on the ground and in the air.

DARING DATA

Jeannie Leavitt became the US Air Force's first female fighter pilot in 1993.

THE SPEED OF SOUND

Some jet engines are so powerful they can push a fighter jet faster than the speed of sound! A plane traveling at the speed of sound is moving about 760 miles (1,223 km) per hour. This speed is called Mach 1.

DARING DATA

When a plane travels faster than sound,
it's said to be traveling at supersonic speed.

When a fighter jet travels at the speed of sound, waves of air gather in front of it. They press together. In order to travel faster than the speed of sound, the plane has to break through this "shock wave."

DARING DATA

An aircraft that travels faster than fives times the speed of sound, or Mach 5, is said to be "hypersonic."

When the fighter jet moves through the waves, it makes the sound waves spread out. If you're the pilot of the jet, you hear a very loud noise called a sonic boom. People on the ground may hear the boom, too!

DARING DATA

Sonic booms usually reach the ground 2 to 60 seconds after the jet flies over.

CATAPULTED!

Some fighter jets don't take off from the ground. They take off from the deck of a huge ship called an aircraft carrier. The deck isn't long enough for a normal takeoff. The carrier uses a kind of **catapult** that shoots the aircraft forward!

attaching catapult

DARING DATA

A catapult can shoot a fighter jet from 0 to 165 miles (266 km) per hour in under 2 seconds.

FIGHTING FORCES

When in the air, fighter jet pilots make tight turns and other movements to chase the enemy. These are called basic fighter maneuvers. They can be very dangerous, especially for people who have never flown before.

DARING DATA

The F/A in a fighter jet's name, such as the F/A-18, means "fighter-attack." That means it's built for both air and ground **combat**.

F/A-18 Hornet in a vertical climb

Fighter jet pilots need to worry about the amount of G-force on their body. G-force is the force of **gravity** on a body. The force of gravity at Earth's surface is 1 G. In a fighter jet, pilots may experience 7 Gs!

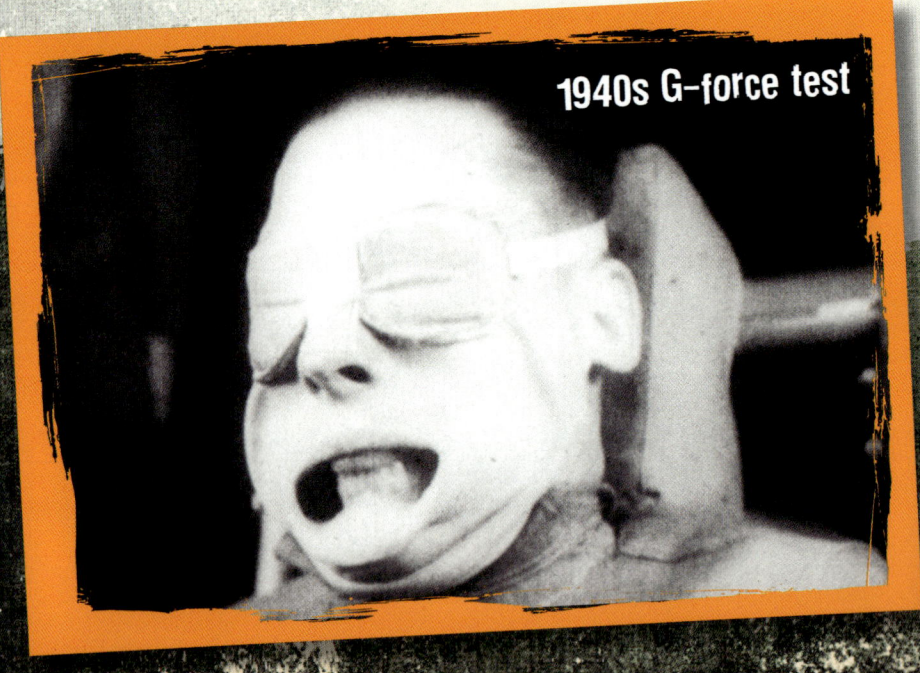

1940s G-force test

DARING DATA

Most untrained people fall **unconscious** when G-forces are over 3 Gs. Their body can't pump enough blood to their brain.

EJECTION SEAT

What if something goes wrong in a fighter jet? The pilot could **eject**! When an ejection handle is pulled, the part of the craft over the pilot is blown apart. A rocket under the ejection seat shoots the pilot up and out of the plane.

DARING DATA

An ejection seat is often rocketed more than 100 feet (30 m) into the air.

In the air, the ejection seat disconnects from the body and opens a **parachute**. Unfortunately, pilots are often badly **injured** using the ejection seat. A pilot in an ejection seat may feel forces more than 15 times the normal force of gravity!

DARING DATA

The force of the ejection seat can knock the pilot unconscious.

ARE YOU READY?

You can also see fighter jets up close at an airshow. People can experience a fighter jet flight in a trainer aircraft, too. The pilot is in control, so you can just sit back and feel the G-forces. Would you dare?

DARING DATA

Pilots wear special suits to deal with G-forces. They also breathe in a certain way.

FAST MILITARY PLANES

Name: F-35 Lightning II
Top Speed: Mach 1.6

Name: F-15 Eagle
Top Speed: Mach 2.5

Name: Sukhoi Su-27
Top Speed: Mach 2.35

Name: Mikoyan MiG-31 Foxhound
Top Speed: Mach 2.83

Name: Lockheed YF-12
Top Speed: Mach 3.2

Name: SR-71 Blackbird
Top Speed: Mach 3.3

Name: X-15
Top Speed: Mach 6.72

FOR MORE INFORMATION

BOOKS

Bodden, Valerie. *Fighter Jets*. Mankato, MN: Creative Education, 2011.

Morey, Allan. *Fighter Jets*. Minneapolis, MN: Bullfrog Books, 2015.

Trumbauer, Lisa. *Fighter Jet*. Chicago, IL: Raintree, 2008.

WEBSITES

How Does a Jet Engine Work?
www.grc.nasa.gov/www/k-12/UEET/StudentSite/engines.html
Read about the many parts of an engine.

How F-15s Work
science.howstuffworks.com/f-15.htm
Find out more about this cool jet.

Publisher's note to educators and parents: Our editors have carefully reviewed these websites to ensure that they are suitable for students. Many websites change frequently, however, and we cannot guarantee that a site's future contents will continue to meet our high standards of quality and educational value. Be advised that students should be closely supervised whenever they access the Internet.

GLOSSARY

bomb: an object that is made to explode to harm people or things

catapult: a tool for sending off an airplane from the deck of an aircraft carrier

combat: active fighting, especially in a war

eject: to use a special tool that throws you out and away from an airplane in an emergency

experience: to have something happen to you. Also, the thing that happens.

gravity: the force that causes things to fall toward Earth

injured: harmed

parachute: a tool made of cloth that is fastened to people and allows them to fall slowly and land safely after they have been dropped from an aircraft

unconscious: not awake, especially because of an injury

INDEX

aircraft carrier 18
bombs 6
catapult 18, 19
ejection seat 24, 25, 26, 27
F-15 5

G-force 22, 23, 28, 29
gravity 22, 26
Gs 22, 23
jet engines 8, 9, 12
Leavitt, Jeannie 11
pilots 10, 11, 16, 20, 22, 24, 26, 27, 28, 29

sonic boom 16, 17
speed of sound 12, 13, 14, 15
thrust 8